This book belongs to

....

....

This edition first published in 2017 by Alligator Products Ltd.
Cupcake is an imprint of Alligator Products Ltd.
2nd Floor, 314 Regents Park Road London N3 2JX.

Written by Robert Pearce
Illustrated by Jacqueline East

Printed in China   0589

Mr Wrinkles

cupcake

Mr Wrinkles was an elephant, and not just any elephant, he was the oldest, wisest elephant in all of Africa.

He knew the names of all the other animals for miles around because, let's not forget, an elephant never forgets.

Mr Wrinkles made the same long journey out to the waterhole each day. He spoke to all the brightly coloured birds who told him about the things they had seen on their travels. They told him about the lions out on the plain and the crocodiles who were making a nuisance of themselves in the river again.

He spoke to the giraffes who were already munching on their breakfast – it was their favourite: acacia leaves. They told him about the morning before the sun had risen and were kind enough to share some of their leaves with him.

Mr Wrinkles enjoyed having his breakfast at the waterhole very much, but could not stay long. He had to walk a long way to see his friend Mr Cheetah.

On his way, Mr Wrinkles felt the ground move beneath him and before he knew it, he was stuck in a big hole. Being wise, he did not panic. He knew that there must be a way out, he just had to think. He had a long look around to see who was there and moved his legs a little.

The hole was deep and cold and came up to his middle. After a few minutes, he decided to call out for help.

"HELP ME!" he shouted. "I AM STUCK IN A HOLE AND CANNOT MOVE.'"

He wiggled some more until finally he decided to stop and wait for someone to arrive. Very soon, a tiny head appeared. It was a meerkat named Eddie.

"Hello Mr Wrinkles. I was just out playing with my brothers and sisters and thought I heard something. Do you need a hand?"

"I do, my friend. Could you help me get out of this hole please?"

Just then, another tiny head appeared, then another and another until he was completely surrounded by meerkats. Mr Wrinkles knew all their names, but could not say hello to everyone. It would take far too long.

"Hello everyone," he said. "Please could you help me? I am stuck." "But how can we help you? You are so big and we are so small." someone said.

"Don't you worry," Eddie said. "I have an idea. There are lots of us. We will find someone to get you out of there."

Eddie and all his brothers and sisters began to spread out in search of help.

It was not long until they found three giraffes called Spot, Speckle and Freckle who were more than happy to help their old friend.

The giraffes, with their long necks, each pulled a branch down from a nearby tree and told Mr Wrinkles to hold on tight.

He wrapped his trunk around the long branches and with a heave and a roar, he pulled as hard as he could.

But he moved just a little.

They stopped to rest because it was a very hot day.

As they tried to decide what to do a hundred
birds of all different colours flew down from the
bright sky to sit on his back.

They flapped their wings with all their might
to try to lift him while he pulled again with his
long trunk and he moved a little bit more.

A few hours later, as Mr Wrinkles was thinking he would never get out, a big wildebeest called Clive, with long, pointy horns, found the group.

"Hello Mr Wrinkles, I heard a hornbill saying that you were stuck. Can I offer you my assistance?"

"Oh, yes please. Clive would appreciate it very much."

Clive stood behind
Mr Wrinkles and
together they
flapped and
pulled and
cheered and
pushed
until...

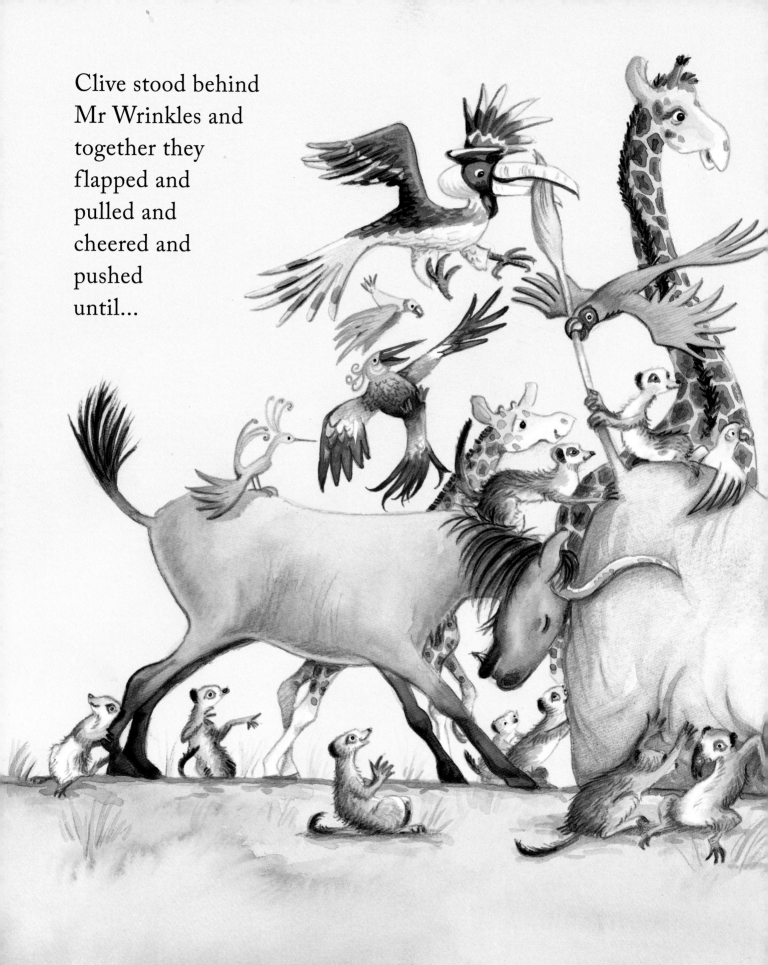

...with a shout and a roar, Mr Wrinkles climbed out of the hole.

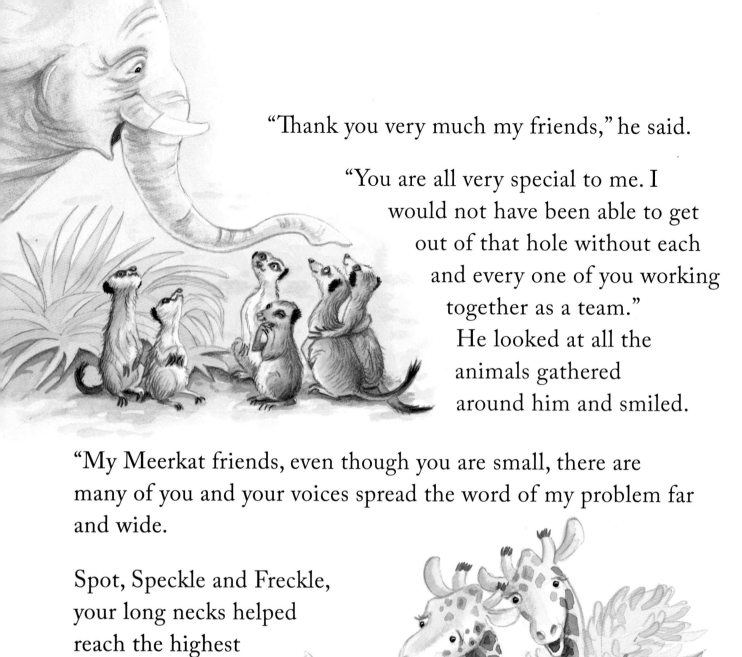

"Thank you very much my friends," he said.

"You are all very special to me. I would not have been able to get out of that hole without each and every one of you working together as a team."
He looked at all the animals gathered around him and smiled.

"My Meerkat friends, even though you are small, there are many of you and your voices spread the word of my problem far and wide.

Spot, Speckle and Freckle, your long necks helped reach the highest branches for me to hold on to.

My bird friends, even though you are not very strong, together your wings are stronger than the strongest lion.

And finally, Clive, my good wildebeest friend, you are fast and strong."

"Thank you everyone for being such good friends. Even though all of you are different, you are all very special indeed. This is a day I will never forget."

Mr Wrinkles celebrated that evening with all his friends and thanked them and promised that he would always be there if they ever fell into a hole.

The End